For Olivia and her lovely mum, Lisa
—T.P.

For Crista
—J.S.

First published in Great Britain by Doubleday, an imprint of
Random House Children's Books, 2009
Printed in January 2010 in Singapore by Tien Wah Press (Pte) Ltd.
First American edition, 2009
3 5 7 9 10 8 6 4 2

www.fsgkidsbooks.com

Library of Congress Cataloging-in-Publication Data
Pym, Tasha.
    Have you ever seen a sneep? / Tasha Pym ; pictures by Joel Stewart.— 1st American ed.
       p. cm.
    Summary: Rhyming text asks the reader if certain unusual—and unpleasant—creatures
live nearby.
    ISBN: 978-0-374-32868-9
    [1. Stories in rhyme. 2. Imaginary creatures—Fiction.] I. Stewart, Joel, ill.
II. Title.

PZ8.3.P995 Hav 2009
[E]—dc22

                                                                            2008042985

Have You Ever Seen a SNEEP?

Tasha Pym

Pictures by
Joel Stewart

FARRAR, STRAUS AND GIROUX / NEW YORK

Have you ever set out
a picnic in a truly
splendid spot,

turned your back
    for just one second . . .

. . . to find a Sneep
has pinched the lot?

Have you ever wanted some quiet,
a little time to read a book,

settled down beneath a tree . . .

. . . to have it
ruined by a Snook?

Well then, perhaps you've been
down by a stream,
playing on a rope,

swung out
and over the water . . .

. . . and straight down
a Grullock's throat?

Surely you've spied a Floon and thought,
"Of all the curious things!"

Gone in to take a closer look . . .

. . . and discovered
that it springs?

You simply *must* have been out walking then,
maybe whistling as you do,

just going about your business . . .

. . . and been chased
home by a Knoo?

Where you live there are no Sneeps

or Snooks?

No Grullocks?

No Floons?

No Knoo?

Well then, I hope that you
won't mind, because . . .

. . . I'm coming
to live with you!